THE DAY THE DUCKS WENT SKATING

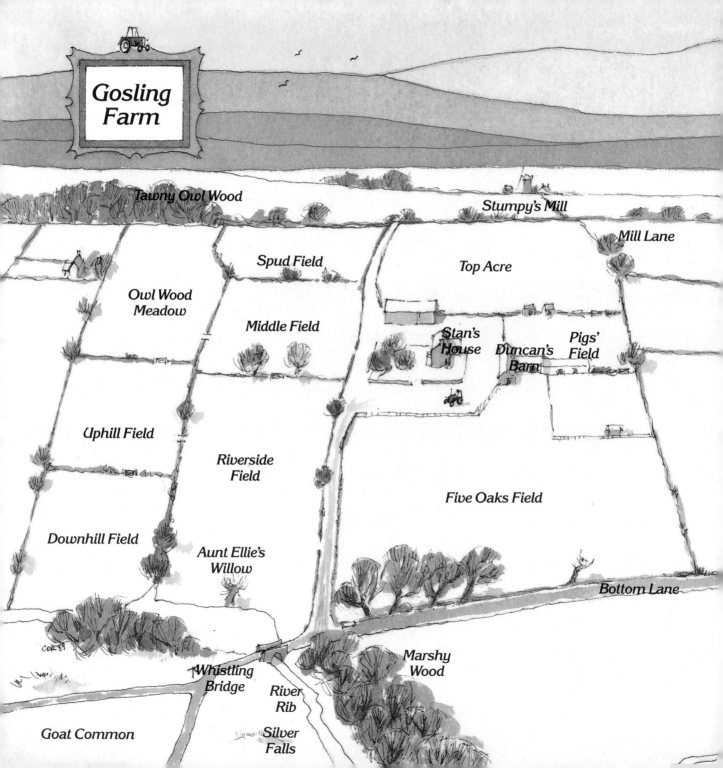

Wrigglesworth

Beech Farm

Walter's Garage

Heronwood Lake

River Dean

For Kerrie

First published in Great Britain by
William Collins Sons & Co Ltd in 1990
First published in Picture Lions in 1992

Picture Lions is an imprint of the Children's Division,
part of HarperCollins Publishers Limited,
77-85 Fulham Palace Road, Hammersmith,
London W6 8JB

Copyright illustrations and character © Colin Reeder 1990
Copyright text © Elizabeth Laird 1990
Design by Enid Fairhead FCSD

ISBN: 0 00 664129-6

Printed in Great Britain

A LITTLE RED TRACTOR BOOK

THE DAY THE DUCKS WENT SKATING

COLIN REEDER

Text by Elizabeth Laird

PictureLions

An Imprint of HarperCollins*Publishers*

The fields and hedgerows of Gosling Farm were buried under a thick, white blanket. Hungry rooks circled the sky, searching the ground for something to eat, while under the hedge dormice snuggled together, fast asleep in their warm nest.

The pale sunlight sparkled on icicles and drifting snow. It sparkled on some eager pink snouts, too. The pigs were hungry. They could smell the lovely warm mash that Stan was tipping into their trough.

"Come on!" called Stan. "Come and get it!" And they did.

Back at the barn, the hens perked up their heads and clucked as Stan opened the big door. Duncan the tractor was cold. He'd never get started today. His battery felt as flat as could be!

"Bet you're cold this morning," said Stan. "Still, you'll have to get going, Duncan. The milking's done, and we must take the milk churns down the lane. I just hope the lorry gets through to pick them up. It's deep down by the bridge, I'll be bound."

The hens pecked happily round Stan's feet. They didn't care about the milk churns. They just liked hearing Stan's slow, kind voice.

Stan climbed into the little tractor's cab, and turned the ignition key. With a wheeze and a hiccup, Duncan spluttered to life.

He'd done it! He'd started at the first try!

Stan hooked the trailer onto Duncan and drove him out of the barn. The churns were full of fresh, creamy milk. Stan lifted them onto the trailer, climbed back into Duncan's cab, and set off across the snow.

It wasn't easy getting down the lane. The ice was hard and slippery, and snow had drifted deep against the hedges.

"Mind we don't skid, by the old hawthorn," said Stan. "I wouldn't be surprised if it's bad down there."

Duncan took it slowly. Fumes puffed out of his exhaust pipe, and made little white clouds in the frosty air. The rattling of the churns echoed far and wide in this quiet, white world.

Down by the farm gate, snow covered the milk stand. Stan scraped it off, and set the churns on it. Then he looked up the road. There was no sign of the milk lorry yet.

He looked the other way. And then he noticed something.

"Oh lor," he said, shaking his head. "There's a fox track, running up the lane. After my hens, I shouldn't wonder. He must be hungry in this weather. I'd best get up to the barn again and see what's what."

Duncan started off up the lane again. His wheels went spinning on the iciest places, but he kept on going.

Stan tried to see where the fox had gone. There were so many foot-prints criss-crossing the snow, tracks of a blackbird and a thrush, paw-marks of a rabbit and a stoat.

Was that the fox, lying in the hedgerow? No, it was only the shadow of a low-hanging branch. Were those his prints, crossing the field? No, it was only the trail of a racing hare.

Stan was worried. He pressed the accelerator, and the snow sprayed out from behind Duncan's back wheels.

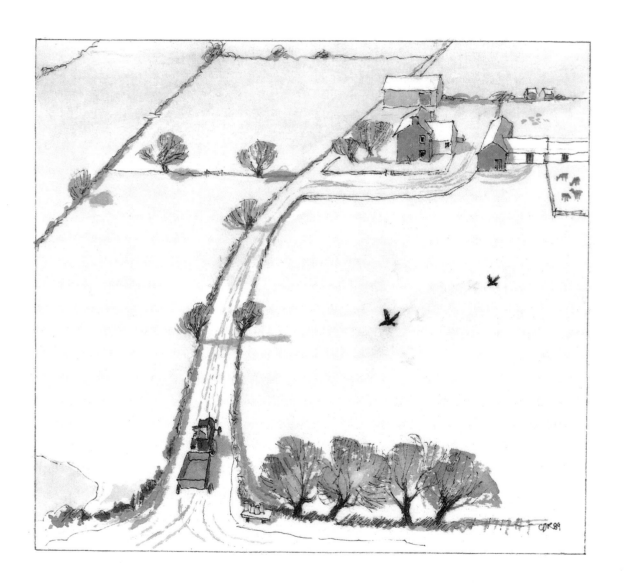

Stan jumped down from Duncan's cab and looked round the barn. The hens were quite happy, scratching and strutting in their usual way. There was no sign of the fox, thank goodness. He leaned over and switched off the engine.

Suddenly, everything was quiet. Stan could hear only the crows cawing in Tawny Owl Wood, and a dog barking far away by the mill.

But then he heard something else. There was a commotion at the bottom of Riverside Field. There was a quacking and a squawking down by the pool in the river.

"That's him! He's after the ducks!" shouted Stan.

He unhitched the trailer and jumped into Duncan's cab. Duncan started with a roar. There was no time to worry about skidding and slipping. Duncan was going full throttle.

Now Stan could see what the trouble was. The water was frozen over. The ducks had nowhere to swim, and nowhere to dabble their beaks. They could not get away from the hungry animal with the steely teeth that circled round them on swift, silent feet, coming closer and closer across the ice.

"Oi! Get out of there!" shouted Stan. "Go on, hop it!"

The fox stopped in his tracks. He knew that little red tractor. He'd often watched it chugging round the farm, as he lay up in Tawny Owl Wood.

The fox didn't like tractors. Tractors meant people, and people meant trouble. He turned, and trotted away along the stream. He'd forget the ducks. He'd try for a careless pigeon up in the turnip field, or a plump little shrew on the riverbank. He had to find a good dinner today, before he grew weak with hunger.

The ducks were glad the fox had gone. They shook out their ruffled feathers, and preened themselves.

Their world was all upside down. The water had gone hard, and the land was white, and soft, and wet. There was no grass, no mud, no frogs, no pondweed, no minnows.

Two old ducks waddled along the bank, and poked about doubtfully with their beaks. They didn't approve of the snow.

The young ones loved it. One tried to take off on the ice, slithered, skidded, and somersaulted, beak over tail. Another came into land, and shot along the ice, cackling with surprise.

Stan scratched his head.

"Well, I don't know, I'm sure," he said. "Can't leave things like this, any road. The fox'll be after the ducks again as soon as my back's turned."

He patted Duncan's steaming bonnet.

"This is a job for you, Duncan lad," he said. "We'll have to see if you can break up the ice."

He climbed into Duncan's cab, and gently steered the little red tractor onto the ice. It cracked loudly, and splintered. The ducks took off with a clatter.

Duncan's engine roared as he rolled across the shallow, gravelly bed of the pool. He'd never done anything like this before! The water chuckled round his wheels.

Stan drove him round and round till the ice was all broken up. The ducks splash-landed with quacks of joy. They swam, and dived, and waggled their tails.

"I reckon they'll be all right now," said Stan. "We'll have another go tomorrow if it freezes again."

He drove the little red tractor out onto the bank and turned him away from the river. The sky had turned grey again, and great white snowflakes were falling.

Back at the farmyard, Stan jumped out of Duncan's cab.

"There's so much work today," he said, "I'm blessed if I know where to start."

Suddenly he stopped talking and looked up. There was a whirring of wings and a honking in the sky. A flock of geese flew low overhead, then dipped down to land on the clear water.

"Well I never," said Stan. "Heronwood Lake must be frozen over too. What a day this is for visitors!"

He leant over to wipe a splatter of slush off Duncan's windscreen.

"We did a grand job with the ice, didn't we, Duncan?" he said, and the little red tractor rumbled in agreement.

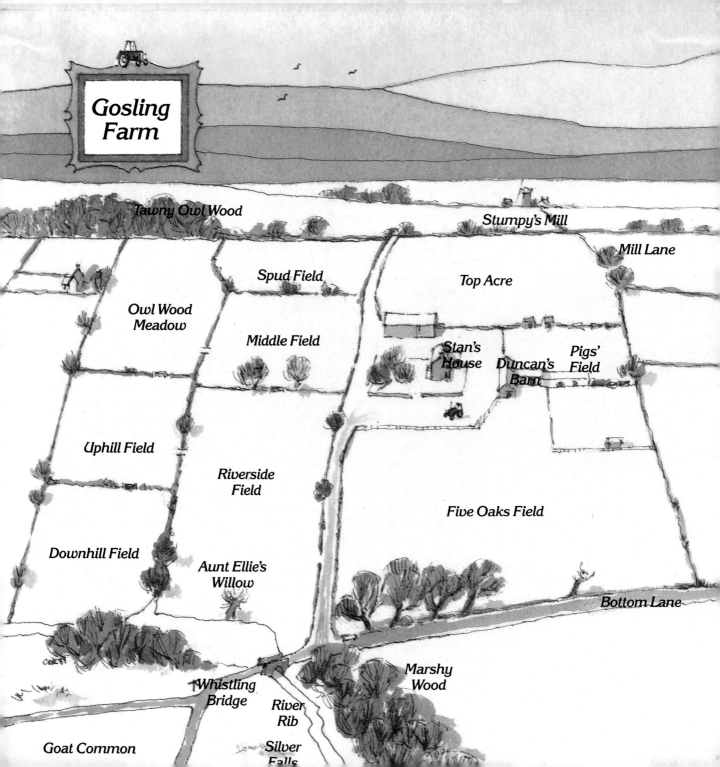

Gosling Farm

Tawny Owl Wood

Stumpy's Mill

Mill Lane

Spud Field

Top Acre

Owl Wood Meadow

Middle Field

Stan's House

Duncan's Barn

Pigs' Field

Uphill Field

Riverside Field

Five Oaks Field

Downhill Field

Aunt Ellie's Willow

Bottom Lane

Whistling Bridge

River Rib

Marshy Wood

Goat Common

Silver Falls

Wrigglesworth

Beech Farm

Walter's Garage

Heronwood Lake

River Dean